To everyone with a table to share...keep making room for one more.

"And all who believed were together and had all things in common. They were selling their possessions and belongings and distributing the proceeds to all, as any had need. And day by day, attending the temple together and breaking bread in their homes, they received their food with glad and generous hearts." Acts 2:44-46

www.mascotbooks.com

For more information, please contact:
Mascot Books
620 Herndon Parkway, Suite 320
Herndon, VA 20170
info@mascotbooks.com

Library of Congress Control Number: 2019916859

CPSIA Code: PRT0920A
ISBN-13: 978-1-64543-182-4

Printed in the United States

Ilina's Invitation

Alexis Glaze

Illustrated by
Ana Sebastian

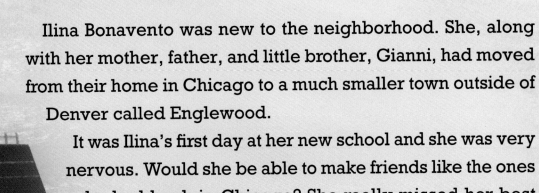

Ilina Bonavento was new to the neighborhood. She, along with her mother, father, and little brother, Gianni, had moved from their home in Chicago to a much smaller town outside of Denver called Englewood.

It was Ilina's first day at her new school and she was very nervous. Would she be able to make friends like the ones she had back in Chicago? She really missed her best friends, Julie and Liam, who she had known her whole life. Why couldn't they have moved to a new home in Englewood with their families, too?

Ilina's mom drove up to the entrance of the school, put the car in park, and turned to look at her in the backseat.

"Ilina," she said, "I know how much you miss your friends, and I'm proud of you for being so brave. You are brilliant and kind, and people are waiting for an amazing friend like you. Be yourself and shine your light."

With that, Ilina's mom reached back and kissed Ilina on the forehead. Ilina told her mom that she loved her, too, leaned over to her little brother in the car seat next to her, gave him a big hug, and hopped out of the car.

Once Ilina was inside the school, she began to feel slightly overwhelmed. Kids of all sizes buzzed through the hallways, laughing, talking excitedly, and racing into the classrooms on either side of the hall. It didn't look anything like the school she went to back in Chicago, and Ilina realized she had no idea where to go. Before she could panic, Ilina reminded herself that she was both smart and brave, and followed the hallway signs all the way to the principal's office.

When Ilina opened the door, she was greeted by a very friendly woman sitting at the welcome desk whose nametag read *Mrs. Golightly*.

"Good morning!" said Mrs. Golightly. "You must be Ilina Bonavento. Did I say that correctly? Oh, I do hope so! I've been practicing it all morning."

A huge smile grew on Ilina's face. It was nice to feel so welcomed by Mrs. Golightly, and knowing that she had been practicing Ilina's name made her feel especially warm.

"Yes ma'am," Ilina started. "My name is Ilina and today is my first day. I was hoping someone would be able to tell me where I need to go."

"Of course!" replied Mrs. Golightly. "I would love to walk you to your classroom unless you would be more comfortable going alone."

"I would really appreciate the walk!" Ilina responded.

Mrs. Golightly led Ilina past dozens of other students and eight open doors before finally stopping at the door with a sign that read *Mrs. Elliott's fourth grade class*.

"Here we are!" chimed Mrs. Golightly. She allowed Ilina to walk into the room first and then stepped inside behind her.

"Mrs. Elliott, this is Ilina, and she'll be joining your class this year!"

Mrs. Elliott practically skipped over to where Ilina was standing.

"Ilina! I'm so glad you made it! I heard that you're not from around here, so I've done my best to make you feel at home. We have two minutes until the bell rings, so go ahead and put your things away and find the seat with your name on it!"

Ilina thanked Mrs. Golightly for walking her to the classroom and made her way to her locker. Hanging inside was a magnet with the word Chicago and a picture of the city skyline. Seeing the magnet brought another smile to her face.

When Ilina got to her seat, she found a Millennium Park sticker on her nametag. Mrs. Elliott's surprises meant so much to Ilina. If it weren't for Mrs. Golightly's kindness and Mrs. Elliott's surprises, Ilina would not have had anything good to share with her mother when she picked her up from school.

Unfortunately, the other students in Ilina's class were not as kind as Mrs. Golightly or as thoughtful as Mrs. Elliott. In fact, they were not kind or thoughtful at all.

Ilina had high hopes for the rest of the day, but at lunch, the other students in Ilina's class did not make space for her at their table. At recess, no one asked Ilina if she would like to join a game of tag or a race to the top of the rope ladder. In music, the students crowded Ilina off the bleachers, so that she had to stand on the floor to sing. During science, no one wanted to be her partner, so the teacher had to assign someone to work with her.

As Ilina recounted the day to her father and mother at dinner that night, she started to tear up.

"Please let me stay home with mom and Gianni tomorrow. I don't want to go back to school. No one likes me and I was by myself all day. I miss my friends in Chicago."

"Ilina," began her father, "was there anyone else at school today who your classmates did not want to include?"

Ilina thought for a minute. "Well, there is a quiet boy in my class named Julian and he sat at a table by himself because no one made space for him, either."

"Can you think of anyone else?"

"Well, there's Lacey in the other fourth grade class. She sat alone on a bench during recess because no one asked her to play tag."

"Anyone else?" Ilina's mom chimed in.

"In music, Carter had to stand on the floor instead of the bleachers, too, and in science, Raquel had to bribe Casey with a candy bar to be her partner so she wasn't left out," Ilina concluded.

Ilina's father got up from the table and went into the other room. After shuffling around for a moment, he came back to the table with four pieces of paper, four envelopes, and his fancy pen.

"No one enjoys being left out. Today you experienced that firsthand. Instead of becoming discouraged, why don't you look for a way to help other people in your situation feel included and welcome? Friday night we will throw a special dinner party for you and your four new friends."

Ilina's face lit up.

"I'll help you with the invitations," Ilina's mom said. "I'll put our phone number at the bottom so Julian, Lacey, Carter, and Raquel can have their parents call me to work out the details."

Ilina got all her art supplies out and went straight to work on her invitations. With her mom's help, the invitations were soon bright and colorful.

The next day at school, Ilina discreetly passed out her invitations to her four new friends. Just handing them the envelope seemed to spark a friendship between the five strangers. When each child saw their name on an envelope, their faces lit up.

Ilina spent every day after school preparing for the party.

When Friday night finally rolled around, the kids from her school arrived with their families. Everyone crowded around the Bonavento's large dining room table, laughing and talking as they crafted homemade pizza crust into unique shapes and carefully selected their toppings. Mrs. Bonavento popped all the pizzas into the oven and brought out warm brownies while they waited. None of the five children were usually allowed to have a dessert before dinner, but this was a special occasion.

As soon as the brownies were gone and the pizzas had been devoured, the kids grabbed blankets and piled them outside on the lawn on the side of the house. Mr. Bonavento brought out ice cream sundaes and Mrs. Bonavento helped the other parents set up lawn chairs in the driveway. With the parents watching, the kids laughed and told jokes together, barely paying attention to the movie.

By the time the movie ended, all five children were exhausted from the day and their faces hurt from so much laughter.

When everyone had waved goodbye and left, Ilana ran up to her parents and gave them a big hug.

"Dad, thank you so much for the idea of throwing this amazing dinner party. Mom, thank you for helping me make the invitations and taking such great care of our guests."

"Ilina, there is always room for one more at our table and there are always invitations to be made. God has given us this home to invite people in, no matter how unwanted by others they may feel. Your friends are welcome here any time, but so are strangers, outsiders, lonely people, and people who don't include us. Every person on this planet was created for a unique purpose and they are all valuable image-bearers of God. Keep looking for people to invite to our table."

As Ilina got into bed for the night, she pulled out a notebook and pencil and began a list of people she could invite over for their next great dinner party. "The mailman, Mr. Johnson next door, the man who works at the gas station down the street, the elderly lady up the road who is always out in her yard..." Ilina's eyes began to get heavy, but she knew the list could be continued in the morning. There were many invitations that still needed to be made.

About the Author

After years of writing just for the love of it, Alexis Glaze released her first published book, *Koning the Lion*, in 2019. Shortly after, she was inspired to write her second book, *Ilina's Invitation*, centered around the idea of hospitality. Alexis, her husband Grant, and their son, Graham, are passionate about creating a space where people can feel welcome, and her newest book is an effort to demonstrate that passion in a way that children can understand. Alexis and her family currently reside right outside of Houston, Texas, in her hometown of Angleton where they have a thriving ministry to teenagers based out of Life Foursquare Church.